Brand-New Daddy

**KLASKY
CSUPO** INC.

Based on the TV series *Rugrats*® created by Arlene Klasky, Gabor Csupo, and
Paul Germain as seen on Nickelodeon®

ISBN 0-439-41811-9

12 11 10 9 8 7 6 5 4 3 2 1   2 3 4 5 6 7/0

Printed in the U.S.A.

First Scholastic printing, April 2002

Brand-New Daddy

Adapted by Sarah Willson
from the Teleplay by Monica Piper
Illustrated by José Maria Cardona

SCHOLASTIC INC.

New York Toronto London Auckland Sydney
Mexico City New Delhi Hong Kong Buenos Aires

"Come on, Dilly-Willy, smile for Daddy," pleaded Stu. "See? Daddy's making a funny face!"

Dil wailed as Tommy tugged on his father's pant leg.

"Be with you in a sec, champ," said Stu.

Tommy held out his favorite ball.

"Oh, thanks, sport," said Stu, taking the ball. Tommy reached out to catch it, but Stu began tossing the ball into the air.

"See, Dilly? Ball goes up! Ball goes down! Ball goes up! Ball goes down!"

Dil only cried harder.

Stu began twirling Dil around. Dil squealed with delight as Tommy trudged back to his friends.

"Your daddy sure likes to play with Dil," said Kimi.

"I know," said Tommy glumly. "He used to play ball and hopticopter with me. Now he's doing all that fun stuff with Dil and doesn't pay any 'tension to me!"

Just then Dil threw Tommy's ball across the room, where it bonked Tommy on the side of the head. Tommy frowned.

"Maybe your daddy doesn't know how to play with two babies like our daddy does," suggested Phil.

"Well, maybe I need a brand-new daddy," said Tommy.

A moment later Stu's brother, Drew, phoned. "Hey, bro, I'm at the Surfside Resort! It's got three pools, and a five-star spa! Why don't you come and hang out for the day?"

"I can't," said Stu. "We're watching all the kids today."

"Well, bring them, too!" said Drew. "Come on, bro! They have a Magic Massager box on the king-size bed!"

"Magic Massager . . . king-size bed . . . ," said Stu blearily. Suddenly he perked up. "We'll be right over!"

Soon Stu and Didi were in Drew's hotel suite.
Tommy watched gloomily as Dil fell asleep on Stu's chest.
"You kids can go play next door with Angelica," said Didi, guiding
them toward the adjoining room. "Tommy's daddy needs a little break."

"Welcome to the Princess suite!" Angelica said, beaming. "I've got my own princess TV, princess forigidater, and princess bed! And this is my castle. Daddy and I have played in it for a zillion hours."

Tommy began to sniffle. "A zillion?"

"What's wrong with *him*?" asked Angelica, pointing to Tommy.

"His daddy doesn't play with him anymore," said Lil.

Suddenly Tommy spoke up. "Yeah, but I'm thinkin' of a plan to get a new one!" he said firmly.

Just then Charlotte turned to Didi. "Let's go to the beauty salon!"
"And leave Stu and Drew with *all* the kids?" asked Didi.

"Didi, I insist," Charlotte said.
"Well . . . ," Didi hesitated. "Maybe if I took Dil. . . ."
"Mommy, I want a manly-cure!" said Angelica.
"Of course, sweetie," said Charlotte. Then she
turned to the two fathers.
"We'll be back in a few hours!"

"Why don't you and I park the kids at the child-care area and go check out the spa?" suggested Drew. "After a steam and a massage, you'll be a whole new man!"

Tommy gasped. "My daddy's gonna be a whole new man!"

"Gee, Tommy, maybe your plan to get a new daddy is really gonna work!" said Kimi.

As they passed the spa, the babies watched people walking in and out of the swinging doors.

"Wow," said Tommy. "This must be where they make the new daddies! Daddies go in lookin' one way and come out lookin' another way!"

They watched a friendly-looking man enter the spa and a grumpy-looking man walk out.

Tommy frowned. "But I just want my daddy to change so he can play with two babies. What if he gets changed into a mean daddy?"

"Okay, kids!" said Stu. "While you play in here, Daddy will be right next door getting worked on! Have fun!"

"C'mon, you guys!" said Tommy. "I don't want a new daddy!
We gots to stop my daddy afore he gets worked on!"
The babies toddled out of the child-care room.

"This is like the time we went with our mommy to make our old car all *new* and *shiny*!" said Lil.

"Firstest they banged on the car real hard," said Phil.

"And then a big machine spitted fingerpaint on it," said Lil.

"And then they rubbed some green stuff all over, and it turned shiny!" Phil added.

"Are they going to do that to your *daddy*, Tommy?" Kimi asked softly—but Tommy didn't have an answer.

The babies found the massage room.
"Oh, no!" cried Tommy. "My daddy's getting banged on!"
"What are you going to do, Tommy?" Chuckie asked.
"I gots to get him outta there," said Tommy.

The babies crept into the room.

"I have a little sore spot right here," Stu told the man.

"A bit more oil will be just the thing," said the man, not noticing Tommy.

All of a sudden Tommy knocked over a jar of oil, which spilled and oozed all over the floor. The man slipped on the slick floor and crashed on top of Stu!

"Oof," said Stu. "I said it was just a *little* sore spot."

The man tried to stand up, but stumbled and slid right out of the room!

But then Stu opened another door. *Pshhhooo!* Steam poured out as he headed in. "Uh-oh," said Tommy, "that must be where my daddy gets finger painted!" He pointed to a window. "Come on, guys, help me up. I'll get my daddy to come out."

STEAM ROOM

Tommy spotted Stu just as the babies began
to wobble underneath him.
CRASH!
As Tommy tumbled to the ground, he
accidentally hit the temperature dial next to
the door. The needle began to zoom upward.

Moments later Stu staggered out of the steam room.

"Look!" whispered Chuckie. "Tommy's daddy got finger painted!"

"Well, red is a pretty color," remarked Kimi.

"No, no, this is terrible!" said Tommy. "He's already gotted banged on and finger painted! Now they just have to shiny him up!"

The babies headed after Stu.

"I see Tommy's daddy!" Kimi called.

"That lady is putting green mud on him!" said Lil.

"It looks like the stuff they used to make Mommy's car all shiny!" said Phil.

"I gots to get it afore my old daddy becomes a new daddy!" Tommy shouted.

Tommy swiped the jar of green stuff just in the nick of time.

The woman who was giving Stu a facial looked around for her jar. "Where in the world?..." she muttered.

Phil and Lil peeked into the jar. "Hmm," said Phil. "It doesn't look very tasty. Maybe I should add some worms."
He began rummaging around in his diaper.

"Now, let's get him outta here!" whispered Tommy as he put back the jar.

But then the babies heard a voice. "What are you kids doing here? I bet someone's looking for you!"

As the babies were carried away, Chuckie whispered to Tommy, "Maybe it won't be so bad to have a new daddy."

"But I'm gonna miss my *old* daddy," said Tommy miserably. "And Dil will too. I don't want him to change!"

A short while later, Chuckie nudged Tommy. "Look!"

"It didn't work!" said Kimi. "He's your same old daddy!"

Stu limped toward the babies. Bending to hug Tommy, he groaned, then stood back up again. "Well, I hope you kids had fun today!" he said, wincing.

"How'd it go, bro?" asked Drew. "Are you refreshed?"

"Are you kidding?" said Stu. "The massage guy flattened me, I got fried in the steam room, and that stuff they put on my face had something crawling in it!"

He stretched out his arms. "But actually, I feel pretty good!"

"In fact," Stu added, "I feel so *completely* refreshed, I can't wait to play with both my boys!